This item is no longer property
of Pima County Public Library
Sale of this item benefited the Library

Hello, Family Members,

Learning to read is one of the most important accomplishments of early childhood. **Hello Reader!** books are designed to help children become skilled readers who like to read. Beginning readers learn to read by remembering frequently used words like "the," "is," and "and"; by using phonics skills to decode new words; and by interpreting picture and text clues. These books provide both the stories children enjoy and the structure they need to read fluently and independently. Here are suggestions for helping your child *before*, *during*, and *after* reading:

Before
- Look at the cover and pictures and have your child predict what the story is about.
- Read the story to your child.
- Encourage your child to chime in with familiar words and phrases.
- Echo read with your child by reading a line first and having your child read it after you do.

During
- Have your child think about a word he or she does not recognize right away. Provide hints such as "Let's see if we know the sounds" and "Have we read other words like this one?"
- Encourage your child to use phonics skills to sound out new words.
- Provide the word for your child when more assistance is needed so that he or she does not struggle and the experience of reading with you is a positive one.
- Encourage your child to have fun by reading with a lot of expression . . . like an actor!

After
- Have your child keep lists of interesting and favorite words.
- Encourage your child to read the books over and over again. Have him or her read to brothers, sisters, grandparents, and even teddy bears. Repeated readings develop confidence in young readers.
- Talk about the stories. Ask and answer questions. Share ideas about the funniest and most interesting characters and events in the stories.

I do hope that you and your child enjoy this book.

—Francie Alexander
Reading Specialist,
Scholastic's Instructional Publishing Group

If you have questions or comments about how children learn to read, please contact Francie Alexander at FrancieAl@aol.com

To Jordan and Steve,
my favorite shoppers
— G.M.

For my dad
— D.B.

No part of this publication may be reproduced in whole or in part, or stored in a retrieval system, or transmitted in any form or by any means, electronic, mechanical, photocopying, recording, or otherwise, without written permission of the publisher. For information regarding permissions, write to Scholastic Inc., 555 Broadway, New York, NY 10012.

Text copyright © 1998 by Grace Maccarone.
Illustrations copyright © 1998 by Denise Brunkus.
All rights reserved. Published by Scholastic Inc.
HELLO READER! and CARTWHEEL BOOKS and associated logos
are trademarks and/or registered trademarks of Scholastic Inc.

Library of Congress Cataloging-in-Publication Data
Maccarone, Grace.
    I shop with my daddy / by Grace Maccarone; illustrated by Denise Brunkus.
        p.   cm.— (Hello reader! Level 1)
    Summary: A father and his young daughter go up and down the aisles of a
supermarket selecting groceries.
    ISBN 0-590-50196-8
    [1. Shopping — Fiction. 2. Fathers and daughters — Fiction.
3. Stories in rhyme.] I. Brunkus, Denise, ill. II. Title.
III. Series.
PZ8.3.M127Ial   1998
[E] — dc21
                                                        97-14308
                                                        CIP
                                                        AC

20 19 18 17 16 15 14 13 12 11   0/0   01   02

Printed in the U.S.A. **23**
First printing, May 1998

I Shop with My Daddy

by Grace Maccarone
Illustrated by Denise Brunkus

Hello Reader! — Level 1

SCHOLASTIC INC.
New York   Toronto   London   Auckland   Sydney

We drive to the store.

I open the door.

We take a cart

and now we start.

We take carrots.

We take cherries.

We take apples.

We take berries.

I take milk.

My dad takes cheese.

"Can we get
some cookies, please?"

Daddy says, "Not today."
So I put them away.

We take chicken.

We take meat.

We take fish.

I want a treat.

Daddy says, "Not today."

So I put it away.

I take corn.

My dad takes peas.

"Can we get some candy, please?"

Daddy says, "Not today."
So I put it away.

We take beans and rice
and spaghetti.

We take bread,
and we are ready.

It is time
for us to pay.

We pack our bags.

"Good-bye," we say.

One more thing—

and we're on our way.